Olive & Pekoe

Olive & Pekoe

IN FOUR SHORT WALKS

By
Jacky Davis
&
Giselle Potter

GREENWILLOW BOOKS
An Imprint of HarperCollinsPublishers

To the Wallkill Valley Rail Trail for many beautiful walks —J. D.   For good, old Olive —G. P.

Olive & Pekoe: In Four Short Walks
Text copyright © 2019 by Jacky Davis
Illustrations copyright © 2019 by Giselle Potter
For information address HarperCollins Children's Books,
a division of HarperCollins Publishers,
195 Broadway, New York, NY 10007.
www.harpercollinschildrens.com

Watercolor, ink, and color pencils were used to prepare the full-color art.
The text type is 22-point Tw Cen MT.

Library of Congress Cataloging-in-Publication Data

Names: Davis, Jacky, author. | Potter, Giselle, illustrator.
Title: Olive & Pekoe : in four short walks / story by Jacky Davis ;
pictures by Giselle Potter.
Other titles: Olive and Pekoe
Description: First edition. | New York, NY : Greenwillow Books, an Imprint of
HarperCollinsPublishers, [2019] |
Summary: Playful puppy Pekoe and his good friend, Olive, an old dog with short legs, have different approaches
as they enjoy a visit to the park, get caught in a thunderstorm, meet a chipmunk, and face a bully.
Identifiers: LCCN 2018006880 | ISBN 9780062573100 (hardcover)
Subjects: | CYAC: Friendship—Fiction. | Dogs—Fiction. |
Animals—Infancy—Fiction.
Classification: LCC PZ7.D288476 Oli 2019 |
DDC [E]—dc23 LC record available at https://lccn.loc.gov/2018006880

19 20 21 22 23 SCP 10 9 8 7 6 5 4 3 2 1
First Edition

GREENWILLOW BOOKS

Contents

Walk One

Olive and Pekoe
Take a Walk in the Woods

Pekoe is a bouncy puppy who loves to run.

He would really like it if his good friend,

Olive, would hurry and catch up with him.

Olive is an old dog with very short legs.

She feels quite sure that her good friend,

Pekoe, ought to slow down and wait for her.

Pekoe adores playing with sticks.
He likes bugs and rocks, too.

Olive prefers resting
in the mud and grass.

When Pekoe finds a good stick,
he brings it to Olive.

Olive just looks at it,
but she appreciates the gesture.

It's time for a snack!
wags Pekoe.

It certainly is,
agrees Olive.

Walk Two

Olive and Pekoe
Get Caught in a Thunderstorm

When the clouds darken and rumble with thunder,

Pekoe shudders and aims one brave bark

at the noisy sky.

A sharp wind blasts Olive.

She regrets leaving home on this stormy day.

Cold sheets of rain
drench Pekoe's fur.
Stunned at this terrible
turn of events,
he hides behind a bush.

Olive feels water
pouring down her back
and is very unhappy.

Pekoe is soaking wet
and tries to shake off every
drop of water that is on him.

Olive is ready to go home
to her cozy pillow.

With soggy ears and
a sagging tail,
Pekoe says, *Good-bye,
Olive, enjoy your pillow.*

Olive blinks the rain away
from her eyes.
Thank you, Pekoe.

Walk Three

Olive and Pekoe
Meet a Chipmunk

Olive is not impressed to see
a chipmunk darting through the leaves.

Pekoe can't believe how great it is
that the world has chipmunks in it!

Olive sits in the soft leaves
and watches the excitement.

Pekoe runs in circles.
Where did the chipmunk go?

Olive isn't overly concerned
about the chipmunk's whereabouts.

Pekoe is confused.
What if he never sees
another chipmunk again?

Olive knows that
there are many more
chipmunks in the forest.

Pekoe cannot wait
to meet another chipmunk.

Walk Four

Olive and Pekoe
Go to the Dog Park and Encounter a Bully

Pekoe is amazed by the many different dogs and smells at the dog park.

Olive can observe the dogs perfectly from her shady spot.

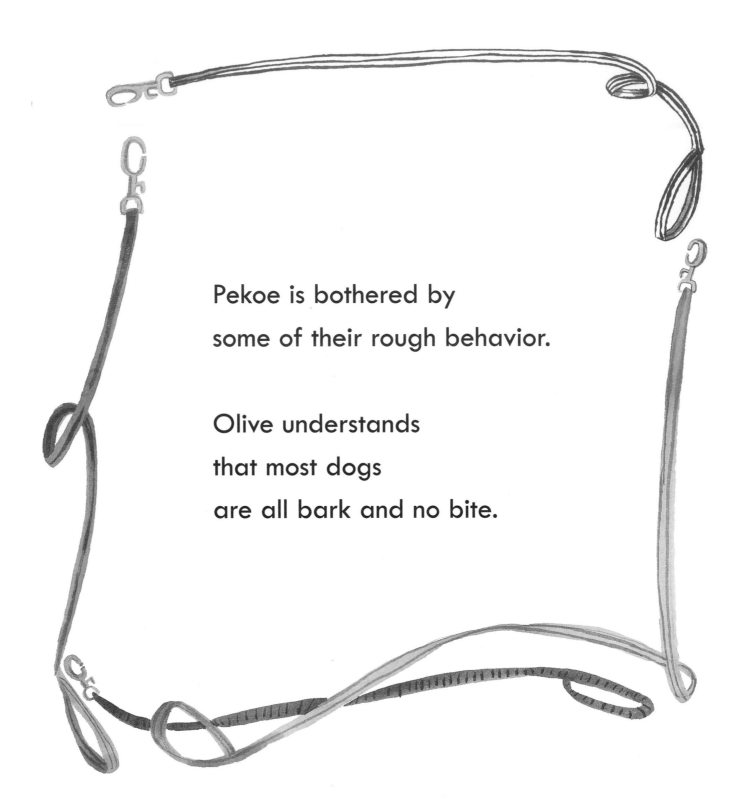

Pekoe is bothered by
some of their rough behavior.

Olive understands
that most dogs
are all bark and no bite.

Pekoe attempts to get away
from a mean dog,
but the dog blocks his path.

Olive sees that Pekoe is upset,
and she quickly walks over
to show her friend that
she is there for him.

Pekoe is relieved when the bully
leaves him alone.

Olive shows Pekoe the place
where she'd been sitting
and asks him to join her there.

They sit together
and enjoy the day . . .

as good friends do.